MATED BY MOTHMAN

MATED BY MOTHMAN

A Mothman Erotica novella

TERRI STERN

Chapter 1

The trees sighed and wept dying leaves in the unseasonably cool October evening, a constant whisper of company outside the car where Laura and Mark were otherwise distracted with each other.

It was mercifully dark, the autumn bringing quick sunsets and generally cooler nights, so no one would question why the windows were slightly steamed up, or come peering too close to a car with no lights on. Laura was certain they'd see someone coming, too. A flashlight might as well have been a flare in the lonesome darkness of the trees, and that would be enough warning for them to separate.

Not that they wanted to do that just yet.

A perk of Mark's penchant for older cars was they had a lot of room up front, and Laura was grateful that she wasn't at risk of some sensor opening the door and dumping her onto the ground outside given how firmly they were pressed together. Mark's body was firm against her, half straddling his lap so they could be as close as possible with clothes still on, lips and tongues desperately chasing each other as he inched ever closer, pinned her between him and the door.

She might have locked the door just to be extra sure, but that was safety too. She'd just about die of embarrassment if anyone opened the door when they were making out. Never mind what they had planned for the back seat later on, if someone looked in then she'd likely commit a murder on top of it.

One of Mark's hands was in her hair, holding her greedily close as they kissed, like she might melt away. Every time held her like she was a treasure, as if he'd open his eyes and she wouldn't be there anymore. Pressed against the cool glass, the chill of the window heightened the contrast of each part of Mark crowding against her – the delightful tease of his tongue, the warmth of his chest, the way heat poured off him as he moaned into her mouth. He'd always been warm, his hand hot in hers when they had just started to date, making careful steps towards each other that started as smiles and tangled pinkie fingers as teens. Then he'd grown into his height over a summer, and that dish water blond hair had darkened to a rich, golden brown that caught the sunlight one day and made her heart face plant down in stupid, teenage love with him. It had lasted them into college too, so now they were here.

That was a thought for another time, though. She should be here with him now.

"You're so gorgeous." Words slipped out between the kisses, his breath dusting on her lips. "I could keep kissing you forever."

Her heart fluttered at his blatant affection, intermingling with the neediness of his wandering hands. "You're a sweet talker."

"Just for you, darlin'." He winked, barely visible in the low light, and she couldn't help but laugh at the way he let his accent slip out. He knew she liked the hint of drawl he had, a hangover of growing up further South before his family had moved into their college town, but it was always a thrill to hear him play it up. To know he liked her enough to do that just for her.

"Good thing I enjoy it, then." She smiled at him, too bashful for the fact they were cuddled together in the passenger seat, his body leaning onto hers. It was easy to be bashful with him – even in college, even knowing each other since their awkward teen phases and growing into things together. Mark felt older than her. More experienced. He was only a year older, really, twenty-two to her twenty-one and in her year by a fluke of the academic calendar between moving states, but it was like he knew all sorts ahead of her.

"Glad to hear it. Shall we move into the back seat?" He nodded to the blanket in the back, laid out especially for them since neither of their roommates was out this weekend, and she giggled at his enthusiasm.

"You're so charming."

He pecked a kiss to her lips. "You know it."

She pressed him back with a hand against his chest, so she could stoop to climb over the seat and into the waiting space, when something heavy thumped outside the front of the car. It was so close it sounded like it had bounced off the bonnet. "What was that?"

Mark paused as well, frowning as he held a hand up for her to keep quiet while they listened. Laura twisted and sank back into the seat, peering out into the dark as the silence became heavy.

They'd have noticed someone coming up. Anyone travelling would have had to use a torch this late in the evening. The part of the woods they'd parked in was just off a public trail, but it wasn't as if they were right on the edge of the track. They'd taken the long back road up the mountain, through trees that swayed and bent in the chill evening, and pulled into the large car park, then situated themselves in the far corner so they'd be out of the way. They could not be more out of the way unless they were in the damn trees or fucking in a hunting hide, which she was just not country enough to do, no matter how much Mark joked about it.

The wind had picked up that afternoon, the threatened weekend storm arriving in town early so not to miss the Friday parties, but it wasn't enough that it should have shaken a branch out. Surely not.

"We should check that out, right?" Mark asked.

"Well." No, no they should not, because that was how serial killers got their victims, but she couldn't just say that. Even if it was true. "Try turning the lights on? See if we can spot a branch or a deer."

"A deer?" He repeated like she'd said something funny.

"I don't know. I was just thinking about what might be in the woods. Could be a fucking owl, but you'd expect they'd avoid the great hunk of metal that is your beloved." She wasn't jealous of the car. Much.

"Nah, a bird wouldn't sound that solid. I think you're right with it being a branch." He slid away from her and back into the driver's side, turning the key enough to bring the lights on. The inside dash lit up with a glow that cast stark shadows across his face, and she hated that it made him look so severe when she knew him otherwise. But that was just a trick of being out in the woods. Things were always slightly strange in the woods.

The car park before them flooded with two straight beams of yellow-white light, pale as runny eggs but bright enough to show the gravel and flitting bits of leaves swirling in the wind outside.

Something dark lurked at the far edge of the left-hand beam - a gnarled streak of darkness that curled wickedly down like a claw.

"That's gonna pop the tyre if we roll over it." Mark wrinkled his nose, reaching for the door handle on his side.

"We could grab it later?" Laura touched his wrist, wanting to anchor him with her for just a minute, something about that curve making her spine tingle. She was being silly, of course: they were up in the middle of nowhere, and no one would be stupid enough to come out here with no lights on when it was already dark. They'd have seen someone coming.

But her skin was tight and tingling like it did before a storm really rolled in, and she couldn't quite articulate why, but it felt like a weight landed in her stomach. She didn't want him to get out of the car. It wasn't safe.

"Better to do it now, so we don't forget. You know I'm half asleep and hazy in the afterglow." He winked at her, leaning back over to kiss her in reassurance, and that flush in her cheeks was enough of a distraction that she couldn't stop him as he cracked the door open.

Just as he set a foot down, a peal of thunder rocked through the sky, the wind kicking out hard enough to blow the door back into him. It pinched his leg between it and the body of the car with an ugly creak of cold metal, and her heart leapt into her throat. Mark growled a curse, pushing the door open enough to yank his foot back in and slam it shut again, then rain was pounding down on them like someone had turned an angry shower on up above.

It pounded down, sheets running across the carpark in the gloom only to slap into the bonnet like the hand of some unseen assailant, the trees shaking with the sudden downpour. Laura squeaked when lightning lit the whole space up, easily overpowering the headlights to paint everything in black and white relief.

She hated storms, had done ever since she'd been struck by lightning as a younger teen and it left a Lichtenberg figure scar that branched from her shoulder part way up her neck and down her chest. It had become a family joke that it was cheaper than a tattoo, and well before she was age to get one, but she'd never been able to stomach being near lightning since. They'd even had to move house, the roof no longer offering her comfort despite assurances about how rare it was, how unlikely it was for it to happen again. No one wanted to try their luck twice, and her skin itched at the burning hot memory of pain, though she'd never been able to remember the moment it hit her.

"What the fuck?" Mark massaged his leg, peering over the steering wheel as the rain continued to drive against the car. The temperature inside swung wildly as well, though the shaking could have been down to Laura's fear, and she grabbed the thick cardigan she'd brought for spooning in later on, bundling herself into it and shrinking back against the seat. It was heavy, nicknamed a yak by her roommate Christie, but it was great for that in between time of being sex-spent and tingly, but also wanting some kind of cover. Not that Christie knew that, of course. She'd never borrow it again if Laura told her.

Her mind was spiralling again. She needed to focus.

"We should head back," she said.

Mark nodded, setting his hand on her thigh, giving her a little squeeze. "You scared, baby?"

She tried to shake her head, but it was a lie. "I'd feel safer back home. I know we can't.... finish off there, but I'm not getting in the back seat if this is going on."

"S'okay, we don't want the car to be rocking for anything except our own fun, do we?" He winked at her, fingertips rubbing little circles at her knee like she wasn't about to crawl into the footwell and cry, and she loved him a bit more for it. He was patient with her fear.

She leaned over, pecking a kiss on his cheek, and tried to focus on his eyes rather than the roll of thunder rippling through the air. Her heart trembled in her ribs, but she was safe with Mark. He'd always been good at making her feel better. "Promise I'll make it up to you."

"I bet you will." He chuckled, almost lewdly, and pecked an air kiss at her as he turned the key fully in the ignition.

The car rumbled into life; the engine growling a little from the sudden cold, and Mark patted the steering wheel like he was calming a spooked horse. Laura sat back in her seat, reaching for the seatbelt so she could hide the way she rolled her eyes.

She wasn't jealous of the car. It was good he took care of things.

He crept them out of the car park and away from the startling branch that had become lost in the rain and howling wind, then steered them down the uneven mountain track.

The forestry commission did not maintain it well, but what track on a mountain was? They were wild spaces - that meant obstructions like potholes and debris, tumbles of built-up leaves that had turned slick and black with the sudden dousing of rain. It wasn't a great road in the night, worse in the rain. Mark knew it, though, sped up and slowed down as he needed to and took them around things like a man leading a waltz.

Laura hunkered down in the passenger seat, breathing deep so the seatbelt went just a little taut against her chest through the cardigan, her fingers tucked under her knees. She was fine. Mark would get them down the route, then they'd drive back into town and hit up somewhere to go. Maybe a bar, maybe a party. It was Friday night. Even with the sudden squall, there would be things going on. Another flash of lightning made her bite into her cheek but she could grip the soft skin of her thighs rather than shriek.

She wanted to take her phone out and check the weather front, see if it was due to last all night, but that would distract him and it was rude to do that when he was being so focused.

Mark hummed as he drove, gaze carefully on the road before him in the little sliver he could see in the twin beams breaking their way through the dark. Laura worked hard not to distract him, counting backwards from a hundred in her head, her thoughts flitting between different things at every beat between numbers.

They wouldn't get hit by lightning. The woods had so many other things to get hit instead of them. It wouldn't happen twice.

It felt like much too long a time before they'd made it down the worst of the upper road, were onto the endless wind of the long curve down the broadest part of the mountain. Laura had never enjoyed driving that part herself, felt like the long curve was hypnotising her with how it never seemed to stop or straighten out, but that was just the way with rural roads. Nothing was quite like the town.

The darkness reached out for them as they carried on, branches sagging over the road, blustery gusts sending dead grass and mounds of mulch in their way. Mark got a bit of speed as they continued down, car bobbing through the shallower potholes like they were on a boat in the storm.

"You okay?" Laura asked. It was rude to be a backseat driver, or even a side seat one. She didn't like it when anyone did it to her, either. They were going a bit quick, though, and he rarely risked his other baby in the bad weather.

"Yeah, just don't like all the heavy rain. I want to get us out before there's a risk of a landslip."

"Right." She nodded, not that he could see it, and looked back to the road.

A figure was standing before them, the headlights just sweeping up a long pair of dark legs. Then they were showing a thick chest, shoulders and arms with hands and fingers that seemed much too long, like the headlights were extending them somehow, and what might have been, was that wings?

It turned to face them as they were coming upon it, and she was screaming. The face seemed to glow, a slash of red through the darkness the headlights bludgeoned through, and there was a horrifyingly solid thump as the side of the car clipped it, sending it tumbling away into the trees. That wasn't a fucking branch.

She screamed again, that red burning in the back of her eyes like an afterimage of looking at the sun, but Mark was still driving. He hadn't even looked at what they hit.

"Stop!" Laura shouted.

"No, we shouldn't stop. We should get back to town."

"Mark, if you don't stop, I'm gonna pull the hand break. Stop!"

He slammed the brakes – the rain still lashing at them, the wind still chasing between the wheels - and when they stopped he finally looked at her. "That wasn't a person."

She shook her head. "We both saw it."

"It had wings. People don't have wings."

"It's Halloween on Sunday. Maybe they were in a costume. It wasn't a bloody elk, was it? We need to go back."

"We need to go to town and get out of the storm. It's not safe out here." He frowned at her, and she screwed her eyes shut as another peal of thunder rocked around them. This was bad. This was so bad she was almost separate from her fear, a sort of clarity that she remembered from the lightning strike where she could tell everyone what had happened without screaming.

The screaming had come later.

Laura took a deep breath, unbuckling her seatbelt. "We have to go back and check. I'm going to do that."

He grabbed her shoulder, eyes bright in the half light of the dash. "Baby, don't. If we go back and there's something, we both know about it. It's a problem. If we drive off, it's just storm damage. Someone out in the woods when they shouldn't be."

Her stomach curled on itself in disgust, and she had to swallow twice before she could speak properly. "Would you want someone to do that if it was me?"

"You don't have wings. There's no way that was a person." Laura pulled away from him, opening the door enough to get her foot out. Cold flooded around her, the wind biting against her jeans, the ground below crunching as she shifted her weight. "If you go out there, I'm not waiting for you."

That made her breath catch in her throat – a blatant threat, given he knew how afraid she was of the storm. But she didn't believe in meeting a threat anything but head on, and if this was the man he was, she would be better.

"Fuck you, then." She slid out of the car, tugging the cardigan tighter around her as the door thumped closed.

The cold was on her like an animal, slipping through her paltry layers and grabbing at her chest. She screwed her eyes shut, as much to squeeze the tears out as to blink against the rain, and stumbled back the way they'd come.

A flash lit the road for her and she grabbed her own elbows, tightening her grip against her arms until they pressed against her ribs like they were trying to keep her racing heart within.

She kept waiting for Mark to follow her, for him to realise what he'd suggested they do and how wrong it was. She waited right until she heard the engine start up again, and, turning, saw his taillights vanishing down the track. They weren't as bright as the eyes she'd been.

Bastard.

Somehow, she held onto her calm. Maybe her anger was leaking out with the tears. Her phone hung heavy in the cardigan pocket and she groped for it, turning her flashlight to guide along the path. It was careful pickings; the storm buffeting her as she picked her way back towards where they'd hit something.

It took five shaky minutes, but she made it, only one other lightning flash making her steps stall like a wary horse. She was doing amazingly, really. Fucking fabulous for someone abandoned out in the woods after they might have been an accomplice to vehicular manslaughter, shivering with cold and half certain she might get eaten by a bear before the storm blew out.

As she approached the spot where they'd seen it – hit it – she found broken branches and an ugly skid down part of the embankment, like something heavy had slid.

"Fuck." She murmured it to herself rather than the storm, or whoever they had hit. There was no absolution out in the elements, but she felt like she should at least acknowledged how bad it was.

She forced herself on.

At the edge of the road, stood just before the sopping grass, she swept her light back and forth, seeking any safe way down there. When one failed to present itself, she sat on the edge, shuffling down on her heels and the edge of her skirt until she was level with the bottom of the verge. The grass was sodden as well, cold leaking through the wet clothes to chastise her skin, but this far down she could see more broken grass, like something heavy had dragged itself on.

"Hello?" she called, holding her light higher to cover more area. "Can you hear me? Are you hurt?"

The little beam of light found a foot, then a leg. Both darker than the surrounding night, they were flat against the grass a little ahead of her as if someone had collapsed, face first, on the ground. No one did that willingly. Her heart thumped hard, once, like it really was testing the strength of her bones.

Struggling into standing, she pitched forward when the wind caught her at the broadest part of her shoulders. Instinctually putting a hand up to protect her face, she flinched into her ever-heavier cardigan, soaked through and dragging her down, before she joined the shape in the wet grass.

The only mercy was between the grass and the water it didn't really hurt anything than her pride. That was already in tatters after Mark, so what was a little more bruising there?

Somehow, she'd kept a hold of the phone in her other hand, grip tight enough that it was straining her fingers, though the cold would numb them soon enough. She dragged the arm back to like a lifebelt in the storm. Her head rang with the shock of the movement, but low down here she was covered from the worst of the wind and she took a few seconds to breathe. It wasn't getting any better, but she hadn't felt a flash of lightning since she'd started down the embankment and one could only get so wet before it really ceased to matter.

Pushing up on her elbows, she swept her phone around, trying to judge how far she'd fallen. The leg came into view again, off to her side, and she scrabbled towards it, half crouching so she could go – wobbly as a new foal – towards in.

She landed hard on her knees beside them, it was a them, they'd hit someone and please, please let them be alive. Setting her phone on the ground to cast as much light as the small torch could, it left her with a view of their legs and not a lot else, but it was a start.

Tentatively, she reached out, almost touched them, but first aid training rang in her head that she shouldn't do that yet. First steps were A, B, C airways, breathing, check for circulation. That meant seeing their front though, or even their upper torso, and what if they were cold? What if this was a body and she had to call the police?

She was spiralling again. Laura closed her eyes, taking a deep and cold breath. Focus. She had to help this person, and that meant keeping it together.

"Can you hear me? My name's Laura, and I need to touch you to see if you're hurt. Can I do that?" Her voice wavered, but it was clear over the wind.

No response came.

Swallowing hard, she tried again. "I'm going to have to try to turn you over and check if you're breathing. I'm really sorry this is happening, and I'm really scared, but I can't tell if you're okay if I don't do this. Also, this might hurt. Sorry."

When they made no further noises, her heart sank lower, settling heavily in her gut. God, what if they actually were dead?

As she pushed up onto her knees to reach for their chest and shoulders, a crack of lightning went through the sky, flooding everything in sharp, bone white light for what felt like forever.

What was below her wasn't human – something inside her knew that, with that slippery, quick knowledge of survival. It wasn't like her.

The body was large, those legs went on much further than she thought from where she'd perched, and the upper back was broader than anyone she'd met with the way a pair of beautiful, massive wings stretched out across the ground. Almost triangular, they were easily as broad on each side as she was tall, and ruffled with the gusts of wind still finding them down in the ditch. If she'd fallen a little further in, she'd have been on them – might have hurt them.

They were black but had a lighter pattern over them, like lacework on an old dress, intricate and reoccurring patterns almost distracting her from the fear screaming in the back of her mind. Each side had a large circle near the bottom tip, the pattern here lighter and near glowing in the strike's aftermath. She knew somewhere inside herself if she reached out and touched them, they'd be achingly soft. They called to her, made her heart flutter at the idea of reaching down and ever so gently stroking them, but that slippery part of her brain knew she should not do that.

It also told her, as she registered that the wings were not in fact ruffling in the wind but were stretching, testing that they were still working, that she should run.

She grabbed her phone, twisting on her knees to start towards the embankment, when something grabbed her wrist. In an instant she wasn't in the storm, wasn't within herself, she was the storm – was the wind, the driving rain tumbling with joy and inevitability, the electric and glorious forks of lightning that rushed through the air like chariots for the new world. Her scars flared with what might have been pain if she was still feeling her body, but now they simply sang with energy and beauty at the marvel of the storm around them. When it let her go, she flopped sideways into the grass as if someone had pulled a plug from her spine.

Something, the something, stood up, and shuffled closer to her with the cautious gait of a wild creature, and she couldn't move. Her legs were useless, leaden, she could do nothing but blink and hold on to her phone as if it would somehow save her from what was staring down.

It almost could have looked human – there were shoulders, to support the wings, and a face, but it was shorter than a person's should be, and the little mouth was neat, pulled down in a curious moue. Ears, if they could be called that, stuck up at the front not unlike a bat. But those eyes, they glowed red like blood and rubies. Like death, maybe, though her fear told her worse things could happen than death.

It came just as close as it could, the large feet pressing against her cardigan at her shoulder, and with what seemed like a deep breath in, it extended one wing up, over and across her body. So the rain bounced off it rather than her.

She blinked at it, tried to speak, but no words would come. It seemed to know she tried, bobbed its head a little and blinked those terrifying eyes, and when it opened its mouth, like it would speak instead, she went mercifully into unconsciousness.

Chapter 2

If she could call them dreams, she dreamed of soft wings and the fluttering one hears at night, when the moon is high and the sky is bright with stars that seem to stretch on forever. But they did not feel like dreams should.

It was still dark when Laura woke, and the storm had stopped. Though she was shivering from the cold, it didn't feel like she'd died.

Good start.

Sitting up brought a rush of dizziness and her stomach rolled in protest, but she managed it, propping herself up on her elbows so she could breathe, slow and even. The unnatural stillness from after the storm surrounded her, the air feeling pregnant with anticipation and all rained out. Nothing rushed out of the woods to her, and it was almost a blessing she was alone.

She groped around for her phone, amazed to find it fully charged but lacking signal. It hadn't even been fully charged when they drove out. Setting that aside for now, she peeled herself up from the forest floor. While her cardigan hung about her like the pelt of some dead thing, heavy with rain, it also sparkled a little in the night, tiny glints like frost shinning in the light of her phone. She needed to move of she might freeze out here.

Closing her eyes, she rubbed over her face, touching it until it felt warm and real again, until she was settled into her body once more. Whatever they had hit, it wasn't here anymore, and it hadn't hurt her. Not really. Her scars tingled like peppermint tea did on her tongue, and she was cold through, but her shaky legs still walked. She could see what her phone alighted over, so she must be okay. Somehow.

Now she had to get back to town.

Wobbling down the mountain track was easier with her phone light and the wind having dropped, and it took her about the same time it would have in the daylight. There was no sign of the false light of dawn, but far off across the woods she could guide herself by the sodium glow of streetlights from the town, so she walked along the main road towards it.

It was dark enough that the stars shone down like she imagined they must for sailors, way back when there were unknown parts of the world to chase after on maps. The trees that flanked her walk home were all taller than houses, taller than even the church spires at the town - the old sort that had near bare trunks up about a story, then were filled with lush, thick branches towards the top. They dripped and sighed, just like the others had done in the car park hours ago, and it almost felt like she had company walking home. As if there could be someone else walking the same route on the other side of the line of trees, lost to her because of the sheer density of the forest.

On the off chance some other lonesome soul was making the same journey she kept her light on, pointed down on the tarmac so she hadn't survived the storm and whatever else happened just to break her fucking ankle. That might just send her right over the edge.

Instead, she hummed to herself as she picked along the uneven edge of the road - an old song she half remembered enough to turn it into some looping chorus. It might have been a sea shanty at some point, or some kind of working song her grandad taught her one of those endless summers when he was still with them. That was a wonderful memory, and she clung to it, keeping all the other thoughts down in the back of her mind. Mark. Whatever had just happened. All she needed was to get back and to sleep. Things would be better after she slept.

About a mile and a half into her isolated pilgrimage home, the growl of an engine echoed through the night, curling along the road like smoke in the cold. There was no point in seeking to flag them down until their lights were visible, so she kept walking, only holding her phone up and out once the bright beam of LED lights swept her shadow in front of her like a hungry wave on the shore.

The car slowed, drove past her, then stopped. The passenger door popped open, just far enough that she suspected the driver had leaned over without taking their seatbelt off. She trotted along to it, grip on her phone tightening so it was close to her side. They didn't know she had zero signal.

As she approached the door, she held the phone up, shining it inside so she could check the back seats. It was a beaten-up old car, certainly held together with hope and elbow grease more than any of the care Mark gave his vehicle, but the man in the front was blinking at her like he'd seen a ghost and maybe they were both just as scared as each other. She could hope for that, right?

Trying to seem more confident than she really was, she opened the door, leaning in a little. "Hi."

"Hi there." He smiled, tilting his head a little either way. He was an older guy, maybe in his late fifties, with broad streaks of silver at his temples and an open denim shirt that seemed comfortable, as if he'd been wearing it all day. Laura might have recognised him from around town, but she couldn't have been sure, any more than anything else tonight. "You just about spooked the life out of me there, miss. Are you stuck?"

"Yeah, I got left behind up the mountain. Are you going into town?"

"Sure am. You want a lift back in?"

Laura pulled up a little, glancing along the dark road. Getting in a car with a stranger was clearly not the best plan in the world, but she was lacking options and so tired. "I might, yeah. But I have my phone on me, and I've had a real awful night, so if you try anything funny I'll make it a problem for you."

He sucked air through his teeth, nodding at her words. "Right sensible for a lady on her own to be saying that, miss, but I promise I won't do anything other than talk to you. Or not, my good lady wife says I talk too much when I don't know what to say, and she often tells me to hush up."

The comment about his wife was some little comfort, though terrible men could have wives as well. On the balance of it, she was cold and wet and miserable enough that if he tried anything she just might scratch his eyes out.

So she got in the car.

He let her settle in with her seatbelt and looked at her dripping form for a few minutes before he reached back and tugged forward a woollen blanket, well worn and tatty at the edges. "I love this a lot, so I'd right prefer you give it back to me before you leave, but you must be chilled through."

She nodded, taking it from him and wrapping it around herself without setting her phone down. "Thanks, that's kind."

He hummed, clicking his indicator on despite there being no other vehicles on the road. "Well, it's what you have to do, put kindness out into the world. And I don't see no one else about to stop for you, tonight at least, so trying my best to do that."

"What do you mean?" She looked at him, grateful to see his eyes were on the road.

"When I first saw you I about thought you was Annalise Michaels, finally stumbled out of the woods. Not sure most people would stop for a ghost if they saw one, but I don't reckon ghosts come with mobile phones, so I took the chance."

The name rang a distant bell in Laura's mind, a sort of low awareness of something she should know about but couldn't really remember. "Annalise Michaels?"

"She's a girl went missing about thirteen, fourteen years back. You were probably just real small when it happened. She'd been hiking on the trail with family and never came back down after going out to look at the stars."

Laura swallowed, shivering under the blanket. Didn't come back could mean so many things. "I wasn't here then, but I think I remember a memorial when I moved, like a vigil."

"Yes, her family used to hold a candlelight vigil. Stopped after five years or so." The year after Laura's family got into town then. No wonder the memory hadn't stuck. "It's a crying shame, of course. But, wicked as it is for me to say, I'm mighty glad you were you and not her. I might say my prayers extra careful tonight."

"Might be a good night for that, yeah." Laura shook her head, taking a deep breath. It didn't feel like prayers would have helped her. Maybe nothing would. At least the shock seemed to be lasting long enough to get her back home. "I don't know if I know you from town, but I'm awfully grateful you were coming along."

He glanced her way, eyes off the road short just a few minutes. "Something bad happened up the mountain? I can take you to the hospital if you need. I won't ask any questions. Can't pay for you, like, but I can get you there."

She licked the back of her teeth, unsure she could explain what happened. Certainly not without making it sound like Mark had driven off after hitting someone, or making herself sound mad, and neither of those was a big help. "Things just got a bit mixed up and I needed to find a way back. Walking seemed as quick as waiting."

"Then it's a good thing I was coming back home. I'll drop you at the town centre, if you like, so you don't need to worry about me knowing where you live."

Begrudgingly, she had to admit she'd prefer he didn't know her address. It was refreshing not to have to do the no, anywhere will do dance. "That would be good. What's your name?"

"Thomas Marshall, miss. My good lady's Ariana, that owns the bookshop on the west side."

She knew that shop, in the familiar way you got to recognise places in a town once you'd been there a while, and she nodded. "I haven't been in too often, but I know it."

"Well, she'd about chase me round the house with a broom if I didn't offer a lady wandering in the rain a lift, especially in the dark, so you can thank her next time you're past." He chuckled to himself, shaking his head a little. "She's never gonna let me live down that I thought you were a ghost, either."

"I'm pretty sure I could have been, if that's any comfort. I could have frozen to death out there." It sounded like something she should say, sound like it had been a normal sort of accident and not whatever had happened. She shook her head, trying to stop the thought from taking root.

"Is there anyone you want me to call when I drop you off?"

She shook her head. "I have my phone. It's okay. But thanks."

The rest of the trip passed in a peaceable chatter, Thomas telling her about his wife's shop and his own work as a driver, volunteering for the organ transplant service after he'd retired. It was easy to focus on his voice and the way the headlights ate the road up, chasing the shadows away as they approached the town.

"You sure you're alright, miss?" Thomas asked when they pulled up to the town square.

"I think I need to sleep, is all."

"See if you can have a shower first, just to warm you through. That blanket will have kept the chill off, but it's better to get warm again."

She nodded to him, closing the door and watching him drive off before she walked back to her dorm. It was harder to see the stars now she was back in the town, and the storm had blown everyone else home, though that could also have been that it was nearly four am.

Idly, part of her thought about calling Mark, but her phone was still stuck as a flashlight and maybe, just maybe, she wanted him to sweat a little.

Chapter 3

This time she understood she was dreaming, because her bed had never felt so luxurious in real life. She was cocooned in greens and browns, flashes of red that brought rose petals and the reddest autumn apples to her mind, and her body had lost all the aches of cold and tumbles from the night before. Now she was caressed by soft silks, the scent of the forest washing over her when she turned on the sheets, settled deeper while her body rippled with pleasure.

Something soft nestled between her thighs, the weight of a body over her legs like an exciting secret. She gasped as she realised the feeling that thrummed from within her was a tongue gently lapping at her, coaxing her higher with insistent kitten licks that kept her clit alight with constant pressure.

She wanted to reach down and sink her hands into their hair, whoever this dream lover was, but her body was lost to the growing orgasm that chased up her spine, and the bed was so soft. It was easier to sink into their attention, to roll with the waves that rushed her towards her peak and reward their sleep-soaked efforts with her moans.

The red of sunsets and fresh wounds washed through this deep, safe place, and she couldn't find it in herself to do anything but give in. So, she did, letting the sounds out as whoever she'd dreamed up gripped her hips like she would fade away into the mists of sleep herself.

Chapter 4

Laura woke alone in her dorm room, her dream lover gone with the sunlight streaming through despite the drawn curtains. The jumping in her thighs told her the dream had been genuine enough, and she half felt that if she checked her hips, there might be bruises from the grip on her. But they could also be from last night. She'd found plenty of knicks and bruises already starting when she soaked herself in the shower for a half hour.

At least she'd had pleasurable dreams to make up for the nightmare of the evening before.

Groping around her bed, she found her phone somehow still plugged in to charge, despite it miraculously – impossibly - still being at full battery when she'd got home. It kindly informed her it was past noon.

She seemed to have a signal again, as she'd got updates from socials and messages from friends about the parties she'd been busy missing when everything had gone so wrong. No messages from Mark.

Fucker. Maybe she'd key the car. Maybe she'd set it on fucking fire. Either way, she'd let him sweat a bit longer. He'd left her up there. He could worry if she was dead or not, and if they'd hit someone or not.

That idea brought tears, hot and bright, at the back of her eyes. She sniffed to dissuade them, wiping them quickly away when they refused to retreat. Really, she thought she'd got all the tears out in the shower last night, but maybe the bruises on her pride and heart would take a little longer to come out.

Her scars still tingled, but that could have been the shower. She was in there a long while, and had turned it up as hot as she could stand to get some of the cold out from her bones. Thomas had been right that it helped. She should take him a box of chocolate of something to his wife's shop, as a thank you. And really, she didn't need to bother a doctor with her scars unless they didn't calm down in a few days. She knew that from when she'd accidentally got sunburn one year. Scars could just be sensitive sometimes.

Instead, she wanted to focus on figuring out what had happened to her last night. What she'd seen. How she'd survived, because that wasn't something she suspected most people lived through. But how would she know? She was studying tourism and anthropology, not wildlife and... whatever that thing had been.

The pattern from its wings flashed in her mind, those glowing circles like eyes mirroring behind the darkness of her eyelids. She shivered, pushing herself out of bed and staggering into the bathroom to splash cold water on her face.

No one else was home, either still out after parties or already out at work, and it was easy to get dressed and out the door rather than rattling around on her own. Staying too long with her own thoughts didn't seem like a good idea.

Instead, she found herself downtown, buying take away coffee she didn't need and rationalising with herself that she didn't need to go back out to the woods. There was no reason to go back out there.

She knew it wouldn't be there in the afternoon daylight. Something inside her knew it, the same way the stars wouldn't be out until dusk at the soonest, but maybe going there when it wasn't outside would be better. Perhaps going in the day would make it make more sense.

Maybe she'd see something that explained what had happened and she wouldn't need to be afraid of trying to put it into words.

She searched up different animals in the woods as she walked back – already knowing she was going to drive out to the woods and just not admitting it – looking for options about what she could have seen.

It wasn't a bear, bears didn't have wings. Neither did deer, or elk, or wolves.

It wasn't a mountain lion because they also didn't have wings and she couldn't remember a tail, but things were unclear after it touched her. Would she have noticed a tail?

It limited her options because almost all the information on the web assumed she would have encountered something normal and rational and not the shapes dancing around the back of her skull like new stars in the sky of her mind. She tossed her phone into the passenger seat of her car, rolling her eyes as she clicked her seatbelt in place and started driving out to TNT point.

If she thought it was Mark she saw near her parking spot, going towards her dorms, she would not pay any attention to that. He could check in with her like a normal human, not just show up and expect her to be at his beck and call.

And maybe she would burst into tears if he did anything other than apologise to her and beg forgiveness. That was also a risk. She was so all over the place in how she felt, at least going hunting clues in the woods would be something real.

The drive out was filled with imagined conversations she would have with Mark about how he was a dick who left her alone in a storm to be killed by wolves, and she was never going to forgive him. Or how he could best make it up to her. What grovelling would be needed.

None of it gave her any answers and by the time she parked up at the same parking lot as last night, now with a smattering more cars while some hikers made the most of the autumn sunshine, she was red eyed and had half a headache from trying to hold back tears.

She would have to break up with him. That's what people did when their loves broke their heart, and despite her compulsion to know what else had happened last night, she understood that's what he'd done. But she didn't have to like it.

Shoving that thought aside, she got out of her car, wiping her eyes and walking off down the track to retrace her footsteps. She maybe should have gone to the hospital last night, it occurred to her as she walked, because maybe this was all part of a concussion. That would be a nice, neat, and very reasonable explanation for what had gone on. But concussions wouldn't make her scars ache, or leave her with the lingering fear that something awful had happened.

That she knew about. Maybe she should search up symptoms of head injuries and check. It could be a task for back home, when she'd reassured herself that she'd imagined those glowing eyes and massive wings. Nothing like that was real.

It took her a little under an hour to wander down the track, between having to get off to the side as cars came up or down and trying to be sure she'd found the right area. It wasn't as if there was a glowing sign waiting for her, but she noticed the spot after enough looking.

If there was anything unusual about it, it was how regular it seemed. The grass was flattened, a little, but that could have been the storm. The birds were less noticeable, a quiet in this section that didn't seem as prominent on the route down. It could just as readily be the rush of her blood in her ears, the way her vision narrowed into the spot she'd stumbled through last night.

Of course she was having a physical reaction to it. She'd been afraid last night. Had been out in a storm, with lightning, for the first time since it had struck her. Naturally, her body was afraid. But she didn't need to be ruled by that fear.

Swallowing again, she crossed the road and went back down the embankment, picking her way carefully along to the spot from last night. The grass was flattened down where she'd laid, strands of wool from her now drying cardigan caught on discarded twigs, but otherwise it seemed like any other patch of woods.

The trees loomed. Grass rustled. The ground yielded just a little more than it normally would because of how much rain had come down, the water still seeping through and down the mountain to join the river that snaked lazily near the town. And up around her boots. Much better attire than her dress last night.

"Are you looking for something?" A voice broke through her consideration and she near shrieked, spinning around to find a man filling the space between the trees behind her.

He was thin as a greyhound dog, with a sharp face that frowned lightly at her sudden leap back. About her height, he was bundled up - more so than she'd expect for the afternoon heat - in a leather jacket that sagged on his frame.

"Who are you?" she asked.

"Gabe Michaels. You?"

He was about her age but she didn't recognise him – maybe a smidge younger, but she'd have expected they'd overlap in school. If he was from around here.

"My name's Laura."

"Just Laura?" He raised an eyebrow at her.

"For now."

"Alright." He nodded, stepping into the little half clearing she'd been inspecting. "You okay, just Laura?"

"What made you ask if I was looking for something?" She let him walk around the clearing, made no move to mirror his steps. There were other people on the mountain. If she screamed, someone would hear it.

"Usually folk aren't out in odd little spots like here unless they're looking for something. And you parked up near where the bathrooms are, so I don't think you're just looking for a spot of privacy." He shrugged his thin shoulders, stopping at the far side of where she'd been last night, so there was an obvious line of exit for her. Considerate, almost, even with how terrified she'd been. He had very stark colouring – pale skin, dark hair, deep and slightly hooded eyes that seemed to be brown from what she could see, but there was zero chance she was getting close enough to check.

"Were you looking for something?" She resisted the urge to cross her arms, to be defensive about him catching her off guard. He didn't know how she was, and she didn't know him either, so they were equally unsure of each other. Just like pretty much everything else since she got out of Mark's car last night.

"Someone." She frowned, the words ringing like a threat, before his lack of action made sense.

The surname. "You're Annalise's brother?"

"What makes you say that?"

It was her turn to shrug now, shoulders hunching under the oversized hoodie she'd thrown on in place of a coat. Just stellar planning all the way along today. "Like you said, people looking for things."

"Did you see something unusual here? Is that why you're here on your own?"

She raised a brow at him. "I'm not on my own. You're here."

"No one walked down with you, I mean. Was it something that made you afraid?"

It would be wrong to say there had been no fear in her heart when she'd seen whatever it was last night. She'd known a fear as deep as her bones. It hadn't lasted though, was replaced with the tumbling freedom of its touch, before she'd woken in the dark. "I don't know."

"You don't?" One eyebrow went up high, and his dark hair bounced with energy when he shook his head to himself. It was very straight, despite the shortness of the cut, and she suspected he might get it treated to be so uniform despite its thickness. "What do you mean?"

"I was afraid, at first. Then I wasn't. It didn't hurt me."

He scoffed, shaking his head again as he pulled a cigarette out of a pack somewhere in his back pockets. "Usually people are afraid."

"Were you?" She didn't know if it was a false certainty that he'd seen it, but she knew he had. The same way she'd known she should run.

"I was." He sparked up, and she clocked how thin his hands were, the tendons clear under the skin. "I was a kid."

"When your sister went missing?"

He nodded, kicked at the grass for a moment before he spoke. "It was night she went missing. We'd both gone up to watch the stars, see if we could spot any of the shooting ones."

"Did you see something red?"

"The eyes? Yeah." He nodded again, worked his teeth against the filter of his cigarette. "You too?"

"I think I saw all of it. I was here with my boyfriend and we kinda…. Hit it. With a car."

Gabe barked a laugh, coughing around the smoke that had clearly not gone where intended, wiping his face with the heel of one hand as tears leaked against his strangled laughing. "You what?"

"We were distracted in the storm, and then it was in the middle of the road. I wanted to check we'd not hit some kid in a costume, my boyfriend didn't. So I ended up looking for it alone when he fucked off."

A low whistle hummed through Gabe's lips, somehow still around the cigarette, and he shook his head. "That's cold. He just left you?" She nodded. "Shit, I hope he's an ex."

All things considered, so did she, but that wasn't something she wanted to face yet. "We haven't spoken since. What is it, that we hit?"

"Different places call it different things. The common term would be a cryptid, like a, uh, monster creature."

"Like a yeti?" She wrinkled her nose, not even liking to say it out loud.

"They'd be in the same bracket, yeah. So would the Loch Ness Monster. Do you like sweet things?"

Laura blinked at him, caught sideways by the sudden change in topic. "What?"

"There's a lot to unpack about this. Easier over food, or a snack, at least. I get really low blood sugar."

She looked him over, how thin he was under the jacket. "Shocker. Sure, I like food."

"Let's do lunch, talk through it. There are a lot of bits to explain."

Lunch? "It's like 3pm." She was also running off coffee and not much else, so even the mention of food made her stomach growl with approval.

"Late brunch then. Whatever you want to call it."

This was marginally less insane that hitchhiking last night, and that was somehow enough for her to agree. "Alright. Did you drive here?"

"Yeah, my bike's parked. Meet you at Cardosi's, on the east side?"

"Sure."

Chapter 5

"I've been studying this on and off since my sister went missing." Gabe hadn't only met her at the café, he'd swung past his house to collect a box file full of information that groaned against its own sides with how full it was.

Laura blinked at it, sat between them on the table, as if it might open up and try to swallow her whole if she touched it. This felt crazy. At least the café's coffee was helping, even if she knew she' pay for it later. No delightful dreams of princess treatment if she was too wired to sleep, but maybe it would be worth it.

"What do you call it?" she asked. As if naming it might make it less scary.

"Mothman. Cause of the wings. I was like ten when I saw it, I fully admit I was in my comics phase."

She laughed, sipping coffee to hide it. "It's as good as anything else. I'd just been calling it, it."

"That also works. But Mothman's been around for a while. He seems to have a cycle of showing up, the longest stretch without him's been fifteen years. Sometimes it's only ten. Each time there's a massive storm, or something terrible happens like the bridge collapse in sixty-nine, or the mining accident in the late eighteen hundreds. Boat sinkings, floods, fires caused by lightning strikes. There's always something then he seems to go away again."

"So, is he causing them, or is he just really unlucky?" Neither option was a comfort, but one seemed worse than the other. A… creature, for lack of better terms, wreaking havoc was worse than something that just woke up with vast changes in air pressure or earthquakes.

This all sounded crazy.

"I don't know. But someone always dies, or at least goes missing. Annalise was the last one. My parents don't enjoy talking about these things, they call it maladaptive coping because it traumatised me when I was young, but there is a pattern here. It's almost always someone young, at least thirties or below, and they're usually caught in the middle of something going on, some disaster or upheaval."

"What was the disaster for you guys?"

He looked at her – his eyes were brown, not unlike the bark of a tree – and chewed his lip before he answered. "Meteor shower. That's why we were looking for stars."

"That's not a disaster."

"Not to us, but to people hundreds of years ago, it was a worry. Less harmful than a storm, for sure, but it's an unusual cosmic event. And this one was the sort that only rolls around every hundred years, once in a lifetime unless you're very lucky."

She could concede that was a rarity. "And there haven't been any big events since she vanished?"

"There was a forest fire about six years back, but that was too soon for his pattern."

Gabe seemed to be thorough. Obsessive, one could say, looking at the overfull box file and the brightness in his eyes that hadn't dimmed since he'd started talking. "And you've been waiting for him to come back?"

His smile was more real, rippling over his face in a rush before he caught it. "I want to see if Annalise comes back as well. None of the others have, but she went willingly. Told me to stay there and be safe, and she'd speak to him, then she'd be back."

Her heart twisted with pain at the thought, at the deep hope of a child left behind, now a young man still looking for answers. Much as she tried not to, Laura could see it. The shape in the darkness. A woman her age, moving to protect her kid brother. Telling him to stay put. "She went willingly. The others didn't?"

"They all seem to be victims of the events. Drowned in their car when the river burst its banks, hit by a tree. Hit by lightning."

Laura's hand went to her neck instinctually, tracing the well-known paths of raised skin. "That doesn't always kill you."

"Oh shit, are you that girl that moved in after getting struck?"

It hurt to have it said so plainly, just like it always had, and she sipped more coffee before she answered. "Yeah. I survived."

"Lichtenberg scars?" He tilted his chin to where her hand was.

She nodded, tilting her neck so she could flash him the pink skin, still coloured up despite all the baby oil and other various unctions she'd used on it over the years. He whistled again, low and appreciative.

"Shit man, I've never met someone with them. No wonder you didn't like the storm."

"I never said that." She frowned at him.

"You didn't need to; you hunch like a gargoyle whenever lightning gets mentioned."

She didn't have to like that he was right, but she'd worked with a very nice therapist to make sure it was just flinching and hunching and not a panic attack. "Rude. So what do you think? Your sister bought the town a way out of a disaster by going with... Mothman, and he might let her go?"

"I don't know." They fell silent as their food arrived, Gabe's plate loaded with a burger and fries and salad and an accompanying bowl of mac and cheese. Laura's French toast and berries paled in comparison, despite being two slices high and dripping with syrup.

They thanked their server and waited until she was gone before they picked up again.

"You don't know?" Laura pressed.

Gabe frowned at her. "I don't exactly have a lot of data points to work off. I have traumatised childhood memories and what I can scrape from newspaper clippings and archives from anything earlier than the seventies. It might surprise you to know our local library doesn't quite have the resources to be fully digital."

She snorted, looking at her plate for a long beat before she responded. "You saw it, though. Him. Whatever."

"Yeah." He nodded, picking up his burger and examining it like he'd find answers in the fried meat. "Scared the hell out of me. I felt like it had pinned me in place, like there was nothing but my fear and the idea that I'd die."

"Oh." Laura frowned, biting her lower lip while she tried to find the words for her experience. "I didn't feel like that."

"You kinda should have. That's one of the common things with the sightings. People get terrified."

"Right. I mean, I was afraid, at first. When I went to check on him, I thought it was a person we hurt, so I was in like, first aid mode I suppose. Saying what I was going to do and asking for replies."

Gabe's eyebrows went slowly up, but he ate a bite of burger and nodded for her to continue.

"Then there was a lightning strike, and I saw him, and I was afraid then. Like, I knew I should run, because maybe he'd be angry that we hit him or just... I don't know. Something told me to run. But then he touched me and it wasn't like fear anymore."

"Touched you?" Gabe's voice strangled through his food, the burger abandoned on the plate as he leaned closer. "He touched you, not you him?"

"Yeah. He grabbed my wrist, like to stop me running off. I think."

"And you're still here?" He poked her shoulder, the jab strong enough that she swatted his hand away and sat back from the table.

"Yeah, I'm not a ghost. Why?"

Gabe shook his head, wiping his hands through his hair before he picked at some fries, scowling in thought. He ate three little grabbed batches before he spoke again. "No one I've read about touched him and came back. No one but those he takes, touch him, usually."

Her stomach roiled, drawing up tight against her ribs like a cat curling away from the cold. "What?"

"There are old stories about him, usually called a forest spirit or a guardian or something. Kids, sometimes young adults, go with him into the woods and don't come back, your usual fairytale fare. The person telling the story says he was leading them by the hand, or that they had their arms linked like they were courting or some time appropriate bullshit. The point is, once he's got hold of someone, they go. So why didn't you?"

She didn't know. There wasn't any explanation for any of it, but that part especially made her nervous. "Maybe because he touched me, instead? Like, the car hit him, but that wasn't one of us. Technically, it was the vehicle. Then I didn't touch him because I was telling him what I was going to do, and he grabbed me before I did any of it. Would that make sense?"

"None of it really makes sense. If it did, we'd know what was going on." Gabe picked up his burger, took another bite while he pondered it. "You could be on to something, though. Intent seems to matter with magic and all that bullshit, and this is certainly in that wheelhouse. So maybe that's it."

They sat in silence for a few minutes as they ate, worry nagging through Laura's thoughts as she made herself chew and swallow mechanically. It was rarely good to be in an outlier group.

"What was it like?" Gabe asked, eventually. She raised a brow in confusion. "When he touched you, what was it like?"

"Oh." A hand went to her scars again, fingering the tendrils that went over her collarbone. "It's hard to describe. Like being dunked into the world in a different way, almost? Like I was seeing everything in nature."

"Did it hurt?"

She realised then that he wasn't asking for her. Not that she'd expected him to be worried about her - he didn't really know he,r other than this conversation and their mutual understanding that there was a something in the woods - but of course he'd worry about pain. About Annalise. Poor boy, left behind to worry and wonder.

She shook her head. "No, it wasn't painful. It wasn't even an unpleasant sensation. It was like, you know when you step into a hot bath after a snowy day? Or when you dunk into cold water after being in a sauna? That feeling when you're suddenly fully aware of your skin and your breathing and just everything around you. It was like that, but bigger."

"Sounds nice. Like meditation turned up to eleven."

Laura laughed, picking at the remains of her French toast. "Yeah, I suppose. If that's how you're supposed to get enlightenment I think they should make it clearer in the teachings, but sure."

Gabe fell into silence then, and they finished their food without too much extra talking. Once they'd paid, and were walking out of the café, he took a deep breath, like he wanted to ask something.

Before he could, someone grabbed her shoulder, and they spun her around to reveal Mark glowering at her.

He looked wrecked – deep circles under his eyes, and a messy tumble to his hair that could have been bed head or that he'd been worrying it as he waited for them. It seemed like he'd been waiting outside the café.

Her heart lurched at how ill he looked: his usual glow dim and his smile missing. Despite how angry she was at him, she still wanted to see he was okay, but when she reached out for him, he ducked her touch.

"You couldn't have called?" he spat.

"This the driver?" Gabe asked, leaning against the wall and sparking up.

"Who are you?" Mark shot, pulling Laura a few steps away.

"He's someone I know. What's going on? You look awful."

"What's going on is my girlfriend did some insane shit last night and rather than letting me know she's okay, I find her on a dinner date with the local weirdo!"

"More local than you at least," Gabe called. He blew a line of smoke out with as much attitude as an angry cat and Laura turned Mark away from him, so she could still see him over Mark's shoulder, but they weren't about to go at each other's necks. Men.

"I went to your place earlier, and you were gone. Not even a text to let me know you got in okay?" Mark continued.

"And why would I have to text you, hm? What happened that I might need to do that? Oh yeah, you drove off in the storm and left me!" She struggled to keep her temper in, biting her tongue before more could come out. "I went and checked what happened."

"I know what happened. We hit a deer or something. I keep seeing it in my dreams."

"Well, good to know that it's at least made it that far, considering you just drove off. I could have been hit on the road walking back in, you know?" She crossed her arms, suddenly feeling small and silly against the weight of his anger, the way he was scowling at her like she did something wrong rather than the fact he'd abandoned her to her worst fears. She would not cry, she'd done enough of that today.

"What was I supposed to do? You were being unreasonable."

Gabe snorted from behind them and Laura shot him a glare, miming for him to cut it out with a finger across her neck. "You knew he'd hit something and rather than check what happened, you ran. You didn't even check your precious bloody car!"

"You've always been weird about the car."

"And you're weird for not checking if we'd hit someone! Christ, Mark, I don't even know who you were last night. You'd never do that."

"I was afraid, alright?" He shouted, grabbing her shoulders. "I don't know what of but I was fucking terrified and—"

"Hands off the lady, bro, you look like a domestic abuser." Gabe was at their side, laughing like a blocked drain and pulling them apart. "You don't want that, do you? Especially when you kicked her out of the car last night. Lots of witnesses in the town."

"Fuck off." Mark shoved Gabe hard in his chest, sending Gabe almost off the pavement and into the road, but Laura snagged Gabe's jacket sleeve and tugged him away from the cars trundling past.

"Even better, push me into traffic, sure. That's bound to make you look innocent, isn't it?" Gabe tossed his cigarette, stamping the butt out. "You sure you don't want to take a swing on top, make it the full scumbag trifecta?"

"Get out of my face and away from my girlfriend." Mark grabbed for Laura's shoulders and she stepped back, bumping into Gabe.

"I don't want to talk to you right now, Mark. I need time to clear my head."

"You're going to defend that creep over me?" Mark's shoulders fell, his lip pulling up in a sneer. "Really?"

"I'm going to get some space while I think about what happened. So leave me alone for a while and stop being so stupid." She rushed past him, hoping to draw his attention away from Gabe and avoid the pair of them escalating. It was already messy without a fist fight.

"Hey, Laura, wait." Gabe trotted after her, waving his hand at her side. "Let me have your number. We should talk more."

She slowed, holding her hand out for his phone before she added the number in. "Not tonight. I need time to clear my head."

"Sure, no bother. You look like you could use the sleep, anyway. You could stay at mine, lest tall, grim, and angry shows up at your house?"

"I'm in the dorms. He won't be able to get in."

"You sure?" Gabe glanced back over his shoulder, and following his gaze, Laura saw Mark was still at the side of the café. Watching them.

This was ridiculous. She shouldn't feel afraid of Mark, they'd been together for years. She knew him inside out. And she'd never seen him like this, just on the ragged edge like he was going to topple into a fury at the drop of a hat. "He said he was scared."

"Sounds about right. But you shouldn't be the direction for his anger."

"Oh, he'd never hurt me."

"Just leave you out in the woods for the bears and the mountain lions?"

Laura opened her mouth to deny it, but she couldn't. That hurt, spiking in her chest like leftover lightning, and she had to swallow a deep breath to stop from crying. Mark was supposed to keep her safe, was her person for when things were hard. And he had left her, because he was scared and he didn't want to be in trouble. She was just as disposable to him as that. "I don't know you well enough to sleep on your couch."

"How about I sleep on yours instead? Dorm rooms lock, you can plonk me on your couch in the living room, and I'll sleep there. If he shows up to hammer on your door, you know there's someone got your back."

She thought about it. There was no chance Mark wouldn't show up – much as she'd asked for space, he wasn't acting right, and she just knew he'd try something. It settled within her like queasiness, an anticipatory anxiety that she only usually had with storm warnings, but she knew to trust it. She'd never been wrong about lightning yet.

"I have dorm mates. They'd throw a fit at a random dude on the couch."

"More than your boyfriend breaking in?"

No, was the short answer. And the other two girls might not be back at all, given it was Saturday, and they'd be out at parties. She didn't want to be scared and alone again. "Alright. But I will lock my door and if you eat any of my roommates' food, I'll make you replace it."

"Peachy keen, sounds good to me." He didn't look enthusiastic, but at least he wasn't scaring her.

Chapter 6

Her dreams, despite her wakefulness, were vivid.

She was surrounded by softness again, on a bed of pillows and pine needles. They tickled her skin, brushed the scent of earth and sap through the air, together with a familiar richness that blended with petrichor from somewhere close by. On her front, she could just about make out a soft bed, blankets and sheets tangled together in a nest of comfort and safety.

It was dark, like dusk just before the stars came out, and though a wash of red skimmed across the sheets, that could just be the sunset. She felt safe, like there was nothing could touch her in her except her company. And in her dream, she knew her company was good.

Whoever she'd dreamed up was with her, had returned despite her coffee based concerns earlier, and they were so gentle in their handling of her. She felt like a precious thing, a gem or a piece of art being stroked and admired, despite not being able to see them.

It was warm, her body covered by their weight, which kept her cosy and soft against them. It pressed her down into the silk below; the material coming up to cup her body, let her luxuriate in it flowing over her nakedness. She usually slept in shorts, but here she was bare, and that freedom let her savour the things surrounding her. A pillow propped her hips up, and whoever was above her interlinked their fingers as they rocked their hips in obvious interest.

A familiar hardness pressed against the rump of her ass and she giggled, pleased at the enthusiasm her dream partner already had. Pushing back, she nodded, bleary-eyed but grinning into their body.

"You feel good," she murmured, arching her back. "I want to feel good."

The fingers intertwined with hers squeezed a little in reassurance before one hand let go, trailing down her body with feather light touches to slip below them both. It teased up the side of one thigh, creeping to the apex of her legs before it began to gently rub at her mound. After a minute of her sighing into that, one finger pushed between her lips, finding her clit with an accuracy she delighted in, and took up circling her there instead.

She moaned, not shy in her dream, and rubbed against the feeling as warmth bloomed within her, wetness beginning to make the movement easier. They pressed on, bringing her almost to her peak before they stopped and aligned their tip with her entrance, the same hand that had stroked her clit settling firmly on her hip.

With a slow press they pushed in, the size of them making her gasp in surprise. Mark was not a small guy, but this was thicker, and though the head had a familiar bluntness to it, there was an unexpected texture she didn't know how to describe. It was almost like one of her toys, not smooth but threaded with veins or something she could feel stroke her walls as he kept pressing further.

Once she felt their hips settle against hers, inch after inch buried to the hilt, it was like she'd never been as full in her life - the girth pressing against every part of her until it felt like there was no more room. She clenched involuntarily, moaning as it sent a surge of pleasure through her, and her dream lover moved in response.

Slowly, he dragged himself out again, until just the tip remained, then he pressed in once more, filling her patiently while she writhed beneath him. As she moaned, he squeezed their fingers together on that hand that was still connected, anchored her with him as he rocked a little harder. It pushed the air out of her, made her skin alight with sparks of pleasure that she chased as she pushed her hips back.

This only spurred him on, picking up speed gradually so he was shaking against her, grinding over the points within that made her mind flash white. Word stumbled over her lips, begging and approval and other things she couldn't keep a track of. It was like everything blurred because it was a dream. There was no need to keep hold of logic here. Of course she could beg for him to fuck her harder while he still cradled her like she was something that might break. It was perfect that it could be both. Of course the hand that was pinned with hers, pressing her wrist down, seemed lightly fuzzed, swarmed in shadows that she couldn't make much sense of for how the light seemed to dance around them. But it didn't need to, because it was a dream.

All she needed to focus on was the panting breath above her, and the soft scratch of what could have been fur against her back, and the demanding, all-encompassing orgasm that was dragging her mind towards oblivion with each thrust.

Something dropped against her bare shoulder, mouthing kisses with scratchy little bites worked in, and she tightened around the length within her as those bites made their way up her neck, to the point just above her pulse that made her squirm and thrash. That was enough to make them bite her properly, sink their teeth against her skin, and that sent her shaking, crashing, into the waves of release.

Chapter 7

The hammering on her door shook her out of her dream, the whiplash of sleep and the sudden awakening leaving her shaking and hot in her bed.

Someone was banging on her door. She was in her sleeping t-shirt, her duvet kicked down the bed and it took her a moment to get herself back together, grab a hoody off her chair and shove her feet in her slippers so she could drag herself out of her room. The corridor was dark, and they kept it free from clutter other than the table beside the door where everyone dumped their keys, so it wasn't hard to check the space. Gabe was waiting beside the door, on the side by the hinges, so if she opened it no one could see him, and for a moment she wondered how used he was to doing things like this.

The banging started again, interrupting her thoughts, and she put the chain on the door before she spoke. "Who is it?"

"It's me." Mark. Naturally.

Her head dropped, resting against the door. She didn't want this. She also didn't like that Gabe had been right, despite her reservations, and she was grateful to have him there. It was a weekend for poor choices, it seemed. "It's two am. What do you want?"

"Let me in."

"No, I asked you to leave me alone. I don't want you here. Go home, Mark."

"Is he in there with you?" She glanced over to Gabe, who shrugged but shook his head.

"What are you talking about?"

Mark laughed through the door. "I saw him come back with you."

"Did you follow me home?" A chill went over her like a douse of cold water, fear twisting in her stomach. She might be sick.

"Yeah, I wanted to make sure that creep wasn't doing anything to you and as far as I can tell, he's still in your dorm."

"Mark, this is ridiculous. I asked you to leave me alone. I want you to do that, and if you don't, I'm going to call security."

He thumped on the door again, making her startle back from the impact. "What's going on, Laura? This isn't like you."

"Neither was you driving off. Guess we're both in for surprises." She slumped into the wall behind her, wishing she'd brought her phone so she could call like she'd threatened. He'd hear her walking off to her room, that wouldn't end up well if he'd invented a situation with Gabe.

"I don't know why you're being like this."

"Just go home Mark. Text me in the morning or something." She hated herself for setting the olive branch out so automatically, for making his behaviour into her problem, but she didn't really want to call security on him when things were still so sore. And complicated.

"Is he in there with you?"

"You sound like a psycho right now, you know?" she called, louder than she needed to be. Her anger was a thin thread through her, ready to snap because what right did he have to act like that when he'd already broken her heart? "You sound like some jealous weirdo who thinks his girlfriend is cheating on him because she spoke to another dude. Go away!"

To his credit, he did, leaving her and Gabe in the hallway. Gabe stayed against the wall, shaking his head. In the bare bulb light his gaze seemed to flash with a tint of yellow, reflecting the artificial light like a cat's-eye in the road, and in a blink it was gone. "You okay?"

"Pretty shit, honestly. You?"

"Scared the hell out of me when he started banging on the door. I thought he was gonna break in."

"The doors are pretty solid." She tried to stifle a yawn, having to cover it with a hand when she couldn't suppress it.

"Bad dreams?" Gabe asked.

Her face flooded with heat at the memory of her last one, and she wrinkled her nose. "I'm just wakeful. Not feeling rested."

"Try to get some more sleep, if you can. We can look into things more tomorrow."

"You think there's more to dig into?"

"Sure. We've got a super moon tomorrow, bound to be some weird shit on the go. But there's a whole day until then."

He was right, and she was tired, so she checked the lock on the door again and padded back to her room.

Chapter 8

The next morning, a text was waiting for her, though she didn't wake until a little after nine. *I'm going back out there.*

"Mark's losing it." Laura sat across from Gabe, who had helped himself to a bowl of cereal that she would not begrudge him in the circumstances.

"Crazy voicemails?"

"Text saying he's going back out to the woods."

Gabe hissed air through his teeth, his lips pinching together. "That's not a great sign."

"Why?" It wasn't going to be a good reason. There were no good reasons left. She thought she probably wanted to hear this before she ate, lest it be something that turned her stomach.

"Well, you went out because you wanted to know what had happened to you, yes?"

"Yes."

"Nothing happened to him. That we know of. He drove off and left you, you were the one to encounter Mothman."

"Yeah."

"Maybe he's been having Mothman issues, too. He didn't look great yesterday, and he shows up here late last night, or early depending on your view of the day. Maybe he's not sleeping cause of the dreams."

"You asked me about dreams last night, too."

"Some people have nightmares. People who see him."

"Did you?"

Gabe hummed like he was testing a note, holding it for longer than most could. Then he huffed a massive sigh, clearing all the air out of his lungs. "Sort of. I dreamed about the shooting stars a lot. Sometimes some of them looked like eyes, as if there was something vast and unknowable in the sky and it was peering down at me specifically."

"That sounds horrible."

"It was, as a kid. It only lasted a year, though, faded off after that. But others, they get real awful nightmares. Bodies, disasters, like car piles ups or the bridge collapse. There's a theory in some places that it's like an echo of the things that go wrong, the past reaching out, that kind of thing."

That kind of thing, indeed. "Right. Not had anything like that. My dreams have been comfy." That was the best word she could give for it without the context of the other things. Her body twinged with the memory of pleasure and she stepped away to make a drink so she could cool down.

"You're certainly irregular, but I wonder if poor Mark's getting the usual experience. We should go look for him."

"You want to?" She turned from her spot at the sink, looking over at Gabe.

"I was going to suggest we go out in the daylight anyway, so sure? Better than waiting for it to get dark and risking some horrible accident on the road."

The comment sparked an idea in her, a thankful distraction from the dreams. "Do you think we could cause the disaster with our investigation? Like some butterfly effect stuff."

"It's not impossible, but I think moths are enough weirdness without folding butterflies in too. And there's always been some forms of investigation, at least afterwards. Police, at minimum, sometimes more when it's things like the mine collapse."

"Those were all after, though."

"True, but it's a stable element. Much as Mothman's cycle is variable, there are certain key things, and the investigation is part of it. So I don't think we'll be upsetting anything if we go looking."

It was a lot to take in, and Laura's head swam with anxiety for Mark on top of the well-trodden fear of stumbling into unexpected things. She's had quite enough of those so far, for plenty of lifetimes. "Okay. We'll go find Mark, make sure he's okay, then see what else we can get. Yeah?"

"Sounds like a plan."

Chapter 9

That was how they wound up back at the mountain, parked up near the top this time, with all those trees sprawling down away from them in the sunlight.

She'd followed Gabe up, past the car park she and Mark had been in, and where she'd parked yesterday, up what was easily a few miles of road before they reached the highest available spot, usually reserved for caravans and campers.

"We'd been up here, when it happened," Gabe said, once they'd parked up. They'd taken separate vehicles, him still on his bike, her poor car's suspension not thanking her for the rocking ride on a track that was no better maintained no matter how high they climbed.

"Yeah?"

"Our parents had parked up here, so there was less light pollution. All the darker to see the stars."

It made sense, and made Laura a little sad, the idea of good intentions going so wrong. "Are we starting from the top and working down?"

"Pretty much. I didn't see Mark's car in any of the other spots, maybe he's been and gone?"

She checked her phone, only the earlier message blinking at her. "I think he'd have said. Before, he would have. He'd have let me know where he was and when."

"But now isn't then." He said it so easily, and Laura was again reminded of that little boy, watching his universe change one starry night.

"Yeah."

"So we start from the top and go down. Maybe he's parked off route, maybe he's exploring that same spot you were at yesterday. We'll find out either way if we go careful."

He passed her a small torch, heavy in her palm, and a walkie talkie style radio. "We're infiltrating somewhere? Robbing a bank?"

He snorted, shaking his head. "Things go weird around Mothman. Maybe we won't need it, but phones can't be trusted. More basic tech, like batteries and radio waves, they're stable. Well, more stable. I haven't really experimented, but I know the reports say radios still worked in some of the older instances I've read about."

Laura blanched. "Does he come out in the day?"

"Yeah, why wouldn't he?" Gabe frowned at her like this was the ridiculous question and not everything else that was going on.

"I don't know, I thought moth meant he'd be nighttime?" It felt stupid to say it now.

Gabe pulled his brows down, giving a brief nod. "I can see how you mean. He's rarely seen in the day, if that's any comfort?" It wasn't. "But yeah, he shows up sometimes. So better we have these just in case."

It hardly felt like enough, but it was something to anchor them together in this strange bubble of time, so she pocketed the torch into her cardigan and clipped the walkie talkie at the edge of her jeans. Hopefully it was paranoia. And hopefully wearing the cardigan would help her, rather than seem like she was taunting him or something. If one could taunt a moth. None of this made sense.

The day was still warm, none of the wild winds of Friday night, and though it was unnaturally quiet all the way up here, it could have been just another day to visit a sightseeing point. Nothing marked this time as abnormal, it simply was.

It was a beautiful spot – sweeping forest running down towards the river, far off, so it was visible only as a ribbon of absence through the trees, rather than water. The town sat even further off. No bleeding light pollution showed in the day, so at most they could have spotted glints from rooftops or the twirling of birds, but little else.

It felt wrong that such a peaceful spot should be so full of fear and doubt, but little had felt right for her since the storm.

"Shall we go down?" Laura asked, after a few minutes staring out across the trees.

"In a minute. I'm just trying to remember things." Gabe smiled at her, turning from the view to look back at the mountain and the trail down. "We came up at near midnight, maybe half eleven. We'd been watching the stars, and then there was a sweep of red, like tail lights."

"His eyes."

He glanced at her. "Yeah."

"Annalise got in front of me and said to stay behind her, in case it was someone up to something they didn't want to be seen. Better they thought it was just her and laughed it off."

"Where were your parents?"

"Further down, in their tent. They'd fallen asleep. My dad snores enough to keep any wildlife at bay, so it seemed fine enough to leave them be."

"Then what happened?" She didn't know if pushing him like this was good – if it was helping, or just needling him – but it would be good to understand how a 'normal' meeting with Mothman went. Maybe he was less scary when someone didn't run him over.

"Next, she took a couple of steps forward, and I think she realised it wasn't a car. She told me to stand by a tree, I think it got took out by lightning a few years afterwards, and that she'd be back once she'd spoken to the man. Then she approached the light."

Laura shivered despite the warmth, and her cardigan. Walking towards it, knowing it wasn't human, was braver than she'd been. It was guilt and upset that drove her on, not bravery. "Then?"

"Then it gets fuzzy. I remember being so afraid I pissed myself, clinging to the tree as if that would save me. Annalise was talking. It must have been to him, saying that it was okay. That she understood why he was there, and that she would help, but he had to leave everyone else alone."

"Did he answer her?" She did not actually want to know the answer to that question. Desperately, she didn't want to know if it could talk, because it hadn't talked to her and she had no idea if that was better or worse than if it could and had simply chosen not to.

"No, I didn't hear anyone else. I remember her waiting for a reply, then carrying on, but I only heard her voice. Then there was a flash, like lightning, and she was gone. Just... not there anymore."

"She literally vanished?"

"Yeah. I was standing there, still clinging to the tree, crying, and I started to scream. All that fear had to come out somehow, right?" He laughed with a practiced sound, the sort that huffs easily over lips with no real merit behind it.

"No wonder you were traumatised. I think I'd have gone mad." She crossed her arms, stroking the scars at her neck.

He smirked at her. "You got stuck by lightning. You'd probably do okay."

"Well, yes." She'd disassociated, and got PTSD, and they'd had to move house. It wasn't vanishing into the night, though, all round it was better. "Let's go. We should make use of the daylight."

"Yeah, we can—"

"Gabe?" A female voice called through the trees, light and full of fun. "Are you hiding?"

"Annalise?" Gabe's face dropped, mouth falling open as he swivelled around, looking for the source. "Annalise, can you hear me?"

"I can't find you. Are you playing a game with me? Come out, I want to see you." The voice sounded from the thicker copse of trees near the peak of the mountain, over the far side of the viewing point and half hidden.

Gabe was off before she could stop him, long legs racing away from her and into the woods with no care for leaving her behind.

Shit.

"This is a trap. This is so obviously a trap." She bounced on her feet, torn between going after him and going back to the car and screaming for Mark because there were still no other messages. None of this was good. She wanted to go home and hide under the covers for a month.

The decision was made for her when she heard an awful cracking sound, like a tree splitting in two. A howl of pain that was all too human ripped through the air.

She ran after the way Gabe had bolted, chasing the sound of pain lest he had gone over or through something and needed help. He was skinny, she could carry him if she had to. Probably.

"Gabe?" she called. The trees were thick here, but like those by the road their lower branches had long since been carved away by wildlife and weather, so she could walk through them as long as she monitored the forest floor. "Gabe?"

"Laura?" Mark's voice sounded off to her side, still in the woods but lower down the mountain, and her heart caught in her throat. She didn't want to leave either of them, but Gabe had screamed, so she should check on him first.

"I'm here, but I need to move. Keep shouting, we'll match up!" She hoped that made sense as she ducked under a straggling branch, the needles dead brown and half nibbled by wildlife, still trying to pinpoint where Gabe went. "Can you hear me?"

"I can." A woman's voice came from behind her and Laura truly screamed, the noise that wrung out of her lungs with vicious fear.

Spinning around, she pressed herself hard into a tree, grateful for the solidness of it at her back lest she faint. A woman about her age was standing before her, dressed for weather that wasn't here yet in a thick coat and knee-high hiking boots. Her black hair was straight and long, just as thick as Gabe's, and her slightly hooded eyes were a deep yellow, like a tabby cat. The light around her was wrong, like she stood in her own little pool of night. Laura didn't know if she could run or scream or just lie down and accept nothing was ever going to be right again.

"Annalise?" Laura asked.

"In a way. I'm some of her, but not all."

Laura nodded like that made sense, and tried not to think about it. "I heard Gabe scream."

"You didn't, actually. You heard a scream, but it wasn't him, and he's not hurt."

"That's good. I'm glad he's okay."

"I didn't say that." She smiled, and it seemed to drag behind, like her movement took a few seconds to catch up with her intent. Laura's heart thumped against her ribs like a trapped bird. This fear was different to in the car, even to the animal, instinctual fear of storms. Her scars tingled, hot below her shirt and cardigan. "I don't know if he's ever going to be okay after what happened."

"It sounded scary, especially for a kid."

Annalise levelled her with a smirk, eyebrows popping up before she spoke. "It was scary for an adult too, but you know that. Don't you?"

"I was afraid." Laura nodded, crossing and uncrossing her arms, afraid she would do something foolish if she focused on this for too long. It was best not to linger on impossible things. "Then I wasn't. After he touched me, he was...."

"He liked you." Annalise's eyes sparked, that yellow an echo of the wings that fluttered within Laura's mind. "You were special."

"I'm not." Laura shook her head, gripping her own arms to anchor against the clawing in her chest. "I just wanted to make sure we'd not killed someone. That's normal."

Annalise laughed, huffing a sigh like a tired cat as she rolled those glowing eyes. "That's not what I meant, silly girl. We all make sacrifices. We're nothing but sacrifices. But the wilderness has already touched you, and he liked it."

"Where's Gabe?" It was a cheap shot to redirect her away from whatever confrontation this was, if it was something like that, but she'd never talked to a ghost before, so this was all improvisation.

"He's stuck to a tree. Terrified, again, which is a shame. I didn't want that for him. But you've made things more complicated."

"I didn't mean to."

"None of us do. He'll take one of you. He always has to take someone. Make sure it's not my brother."

A crack of thunder went through the trees, making the trunk at her back rock like an earthquake was turning below her. Laura scrabbled to grab hold of the tree, plastering herself against the wood so she could cling against the rolling of the ground, and in an instant it stopped.

Looking up, Annalise was gone, and someone was calling her name again.

"Hello?" Her head was swimming from the encounter, pulse loud in her ears, but she couldn't get consumed by her upset. Gabe was out there, and if her ears were right, so was Mark.

"Laura? Over here!" That was Gabe, further along in the woods, and despite her legs feeling like they'd give out below her, she pried herself from the tree. It was darker now, the sun hidden like a storm was rolling in - or like dusk - and she took the torch out of her pocket so she could pick between the outreaching roots, avoid the sudden drops between one elevation and the next.

It felt like she was back on the lower roads, the hypnotic teasing of a circle around the top rather than the bottom. Her scars were thrumming now, awareness on the edge of pain itching through them, but with careful steps she threaded, catlike, through the trees and into a clearing that shouldn't be there.

The trees were gone, swept aside like a wave had somehow found its way to the top of the mountain, enormous trunks discarded here and there with reckless freedom. This would be noticeable from nearer the bottom, a scar on the endless sweep of green which did not exist, but here it stood.

Gabe was clinging to one trunk near the edge, crouched behind it so only his head was looking over the top, and staring into the middle.

At the centre, wings spread in shining glory, stood Mothman. At the end of one long arm, he held Mark by the throat, so Mark's feet dangled freely, toes pointed to the forest floor. Mark seemed hypnotised, eyes open but unfocused. He was limp in Mothman's grip, and Laura was half afraid to interrupt whatever was happening in case it was hurting him. But half afraid wasn't enough to stop her – it hadn't been in the storm, and it wouldn't be here. This wasn't right.

"Let him go!" She ran forward, vaulting over one of the fallen trees so she could throw herself into the centre, be within reach of them even if she didn't dare touch either yet.

"Laura!" Gabe stood, shaking his head and waving her back towards him.

It was rapidly growing darker, like the afternoon had sped up around them, or she'd lost time speaking to the ghost. The dull red of Mothman's gaze was growing in strength.

"You can understand me, can't you? You know me." Laura stepped closer, still not brave enough to touch him but trying to keep his attention on her.

"He can't speak, you know?" Annalise appeared at the far end of the clearing, uncaring about the uneven terrain. Laura didn't dare look if she moved through the trees or over them. "I thought Gabe would have told you that."

"Annalise?" Gabe's voice cut through the air like a cry, half strangled. "Is it you?"

"Not enough of me for it to count. You stay there, Gabey, I don't want you to come any closer." Annalise seemed to leak at the edges, her darkness blending with the night that was impossibly creeping over them.

Laura screwed her eyes shut, trying to squeeze the tears away. "I want you to let Mark go. You know me, you saw me that night, like I saw you. You were kind to me. Can you let him go?" This close Mothman towered above her, the top of her head barely reaching his shoulders, and she didn't know if he was listening. He didn't look away from Mark.

"There has to be a sacrifice," Annalise said. "Someone had to come to him."

"Is that what you did?" Gabe called. Laura didn't need to look at him to know he was crying.

Annalise looked past Laura and smiled, that same stilted movement dragging over her face. "I did. And I'd do it a hundred more times if it made sure you and mum and dad were safe. Hush now, Gabe, you're not supposed to be here."

"I had to come for you. I knew you'd come back, you promised."

"I did. But I can't leave him anymore. I'm not really here, I can just about talk to you because of all that love saved up for me. You've kept me going, Gabey. And I'm so proud of you. Look how tall you are."

"What happens if he doesn't take someone?" Laura whispered. There'd been longer gaps than this. There had to be a reason he was here now. Surely, they could leave. Annalise being here meant she wasn't all the way gone. Maybe there was some hope.

"Bad things. Something terrible will happen to the town, or to the forest, until the right sort of person's taken. He needs company."

The words sat like stones in Laura's heart, the choice bare. Either it was one of them now, or someone else later. Maybe more than one. A disaster in a town now full of students. An inevitability of at least one death, maybe more. The bridge collapse had taken nearly forty people.

"If we go with you, what happens?" Laura stepped closer to Mothman, tried not to flinch when the sweep of his gaze landed on her and bathed her in bloody light.

Annalise spoke for him. "It's different for everyone. You become... more. More than yourself, more than the tiny understanding humans have."

"You're still here." Gabe said.

"Not most of me. We burn up, being so close to the divine. Some faster, some slower, but when we wear out, someone new is called. A disaster happens, someone goes missing, and he goes back into the woods. I think he needs us, as a connection. A bridge between the wilderness and the humanity that he struggles with."

"Was he ever human?" Laura didn't know why she asked it other than when he'd touched her it had felt so purely elemental she couldn't imagine he'd ever been as small as a skeleton, or as constricted as skin.

"Not even close." Annalise shook her head. "Are you afraid?"

"No." Laura took a final step closer, reached up to touch that strange, condensed face that had been so careful with her when she'd fallen in the darkness. "If one of us has to go, choose me. Take me."

"Laura!" Gabe hadn't left his little sanctuary, but she thought he might leap over to pull her away. She rushed forward, pushing Mothman's arm down so Mark's feet touched the ground.

"You already felt me before, in the woods. I won't run this time."

More than the woods. A purr of something rippled through her mind, flashes of her dreams skimming behind her eyelids. She was left gasping from the memory of pleasure.

"That was you?"

She didn't know if that little mouth could smile but it seemed to, and he let Mark fall to the floor with a soft thump as one large hand cupped her cheek, drew her closer. Laura went with him, crowded into his chest as he spread his wings wide, then bundled them close and wrapped the two of them.

There was a shrill whistle like a gale, and a sudden rush of cold, then they were standing in a cave, or some other cavern. It was ancient, lichens and moss growing from every ledge she could see in her quick glances, and layers of blankets and travel pillows littered the floor like a nest. He'd made it almost friendly for people, benches and chairs near the edges of the walls making a sort of route through the place. It wasn't cold despite how she'd felt in his wings.

Within herself, she knew she wanted to go to him. To hold him, and feel him close against her, as something to cling onto.

"Will the others be okay?"

He nodded, drawing her to him again. They will be confused. Hurt. But they will live.

"Do you always talk like that?"

He shook his head, the ruffles of his fur catching the light as he moved. Leaning down so he could touch his forehead to hers, his stiff little ears still pointing straight up, Laura's mind flooded with images and feelings as he connected them. It was like having information poured into herself, a sudden rush of sensation that made her step closer to him, sink her fingers into his chest fur to keep them close. Flush.

It takes time to grow used to me. Let us be close another way.

He took her hand in his, so large compared to how small and pale hers sat within it and led her slowly deeper into the cave. Through a short tunnel she found the space from her dreams, a smaller nest of pillows and silks, a rainbow of colours spreading down the walls in old scarves and discarded shawls.

"I know here."

He nodded, and gently pressed her shoulders so he brought them chest to chest again, before reaching down to grasp her hips. With no effort, he picked her up, and she grabbed for his shoulders, holding tight onto him for balance. He set her against his hips and she wrapped her legs around him as well, scared she would fall despite the firm grip on her.

Slowly, so she had time to pull away, he brought his face down and littered her cheeks with kisses. His lips were soft as fresh dew, a little scratchy with the short fur that covered his face as well, and it was a short time before she did the same. It was unusual to kiss fur, but Mark had a beard for a little while and it didn't feel too different to that, just all over.

She opened to his touch, pressing herself harder against him, sighing when his kissed travelled to her neck.

Mine. He bit at her neck, like he had in her dream, and she panted against his skin, her body flushing hot at the word.

"Yes." She nodded, hands wandering across his back to splay out across his wings, etch over the thick muscles at the join between them and his back. "I want to be yours."

He purred again, squeezing her ass as he moved closer to one wall, pinned her between it and him as he shredded her clothes off with those long fingers. It made her breath catch, but there was no fear. This was just as her dreams had been, his presence just as safe, and she wriggled her hips as he pulled her jeans free, shucking her destroyed top off.

His fur was a revelation of sensation against her skin, sharper in the flesh, but it didn't hurt, and she chased his touch. One hand stayed below her, easily supporting her weight, while the other wandered over her chest with curious teasing.

Playing slowly with each nipple until they were hard and aching from the constant touch of his chest and fur, as well as those firm fingers, he dipped to kiss at her neck again. She rocked her hips harder into him, encouraging him lower, but noticing an echoing hardness pressing against her thigh. It made her glow with pleasure that he wanted her as much as she yearned for him. That the dreams had been mutual, and he had chosen her, had accepted her coming to him.

His fingers skimmed over her stomach, then lower, finding the join of her thighs spread open from how she was clinging to him. His thumb found her clit, flicking it gently like he had her nipples, and one long finger teased at her entrance. She was already wet, shivering as the finger slow stated to part her, clamping down just on that because she so sensitive and needy.

He might have made a sound like a laugh, if such a face could laugh, and began to gently scissor her open with another finger added. His thumb never left her clit, continuing to coax moans and slick from her in equal ease, and she was trembling from his gentle ministrations before he picked up a little speed, sending her spinning over the edge.

Her eyes rolled back, flush with the red of his open gaze, as she growled his name. It wasn't Mothman, wasn't anything a human could say, but between what they'd shared she could get close enough that he preened at her attempts.

She thrashed in his grip, hips chasing the same even, steady pressure he was circling on her clit. Her moans pitched up as he pressed down harder on the little bundle of nerves while drawing his fingers out.

The tip of his cock replaced them, and he let both hands settle on her hips before he began to gradually lower her onto him. It felt like being split open in the best way she could imagine, an impossible closeness that flooded through every nerve and crackled over her skin.

Still sensitive from her recent orgasm, she gasped as he pressed up, filling her gradually inch by inch despite twitching from the restraint. It was more direct than the dream, more demanding, and she clung to him as he moved her up and down, keeping himself still at first so she was used to him, and the tempo.

Once she was twitching her hips forward, and clawing at his back for more, he stepped closer to the wall, pinning her by the hips. That let him move on his own, no longer simply moving her along his length but pulling her into his thrusts as he pressed harder, hips snapping against hers.

It started a fire low in her stomach, shooting sparks right along her spine as moans bounced out from her with every thrust. It was like she'd fall apart if she came, but might if she didn't too, her mind spinning with his touch and her need. She wanted him to come, wanted him to tip over into pleasure and joy with her, but she needed release, needed to reach the peak he was flying her towards.

She tried to beg, useless words spilling out with each grind of him against her, but he understood. He must have, for he sped up as well, gripping harder so his fingers pinched bruises across her skin, dragged her wordlessly over his hardness.

The pressure in her stomach wound tighter and broke, sending her careening over the edge with a near scream, and she tightened every hold she had on him, drawing as much of him to her as she could.

He came too, his cock twitching and jumping within her as he pressed her hard against the wall, bucked his hips sloppily as he cupped her face with one hand. Pecking kisses to her lips and cheeks, he sagged into the wall, still effortlessly supporting her, and seemed to almost coo with pleasure.

Laura idly traced shapes on his back, hoping her scratching hadn't cut through his fur, and rested her head on his shoulder as the aftershocks shivered through her. Tiredness crept across her like the dawn chasing the night away, and she could have slept like that if they'd stayed in place.

Instead, he gently pulled them apart, pressing her to him as he rearranged the cushions and pillows on what she presumed was his bed. Going down on his thick thighs he lowered them together, turning so he rested on one wing and side, bringing her close against his chest.

Once she settled beside him, he stretched a wing over them, holding her so his free hand splayed over her hip. This close, she could track the pattern on his wing, see the faint glow of the circle down near the tip. She slipped a fingertip over them, delighted to find they were just as soft as she'd known they would be, and she let herself fall into whatever sleep would be now as she traced his patterns like new stars.

Other stories from Terri Stern:
The Monster Erotica collection[1]
A Vampire's Debt Steamy Short Stories collection[2]

———————

If you enjoyed this story, I would sincerely appreciate if you would leave a review or a rating! Reviews and ratings are a great help to the author and they make my day. Thank you!

Terri Stern is a writer and student based in Scotland. Outside of writing she enjoys walking and cocktails, as well as belly dancing. Her favorite tea is Royal Milk Tea from South Korea and she dreams of being able to travel again so she can visit there to try it fresh.

Find her on Twitter: @TerriSternWrite[3]
Website: terristernwrites.com[4]

———————

1. https://www.amazon.com/dp/

   B0BVLBV3Q8?binding=kindle_edition&ref=dbs_dp_rwt_sb_pc_tukn

2. https://www.amazon.com/dp/

   B0BTZ4BPR2?binding=kindle_edition&ref=dbs_dp_rwt_sb_pc_tukn

3. https://twitter.com/TerriSternWrite

4. https://www.terristernwrites.com/